ADVENTURES iN MAKERSPACE

A RECYCLED-ART MiSSiON

WRITTEN BY
SHANNON McCLINTOCK MILLER
AND
BLAKE HOENA

ILLUSTRATED BY
ALAN BROWN

STONE ARCH BOOKS
a capstone imprint

capstone®

www.mycapstone.com

A Recycled-Art Mission is published by Stone Arch Books,
a Capstone imprint
1710 Roe Crest Drive, North Mankato, Minnesota 56003
www.mycapstonepub.com

Library of Congress Cataloging-in-Publication Data
Names: Miller, Shannon (Shannon McClintock), author. | Hoena, B. A., author.
 | Brown, Alan (Illustrator), illustrator.
Title: A recycled-art mission / by Shannon McClintock Miller and Blake Hoena
 ; illustrated by Alan Brown.
Description: North Mankato, Minnesota : Stone Arch Books, [2019] | Series:
 Adventures in makerspace | Audience: Ages 8-10.
Identifiers: LCCN 2018044115| ISBN 9781496579492 (hardcover) | ISBN
 9781496579539 (pbk.) | ISBN 9781496579577 (ebook pdf)
Subjects: LCSH: Found objects (Art)--Juvenile literature. | Refuse as art
 material--Juvenile literature. | Recycling (Waste, etc.)--Juvenile literature.
 | Handicraft--Juvenile literature. | Makerspaces--Juvenile literature.
 | LCGFT: Graphic novels.
Classification: LCC N6494.F6 M57 2019 | DDC 745.58/4--dc23 LC record
 available at https://lccn.loc.gov/2018044115

Book design and art direction: Mighty Media
Editorial direction: Kellie M. Hultgren
Music direction: Elizabeth Draper
Music written and produced by Mark Mallman

Printed and bound in the United States of America
PA48

CONTENTS

1 Ask an adult to
download the app.

 Capstone 4D
Education

2 Scan any page with the star.

3 Enjoy your cool stuff!

—— OR ——

Use this password at capstone4D.com

recyc.79492

MEET THE SPECIALIST

ABILITIES:
speed reader, tech titan,
foreign language master,
traveler through literature
and history

MS. GILLIAN
TEACHER - LIBRARIAN

MEET THE STUDENTS

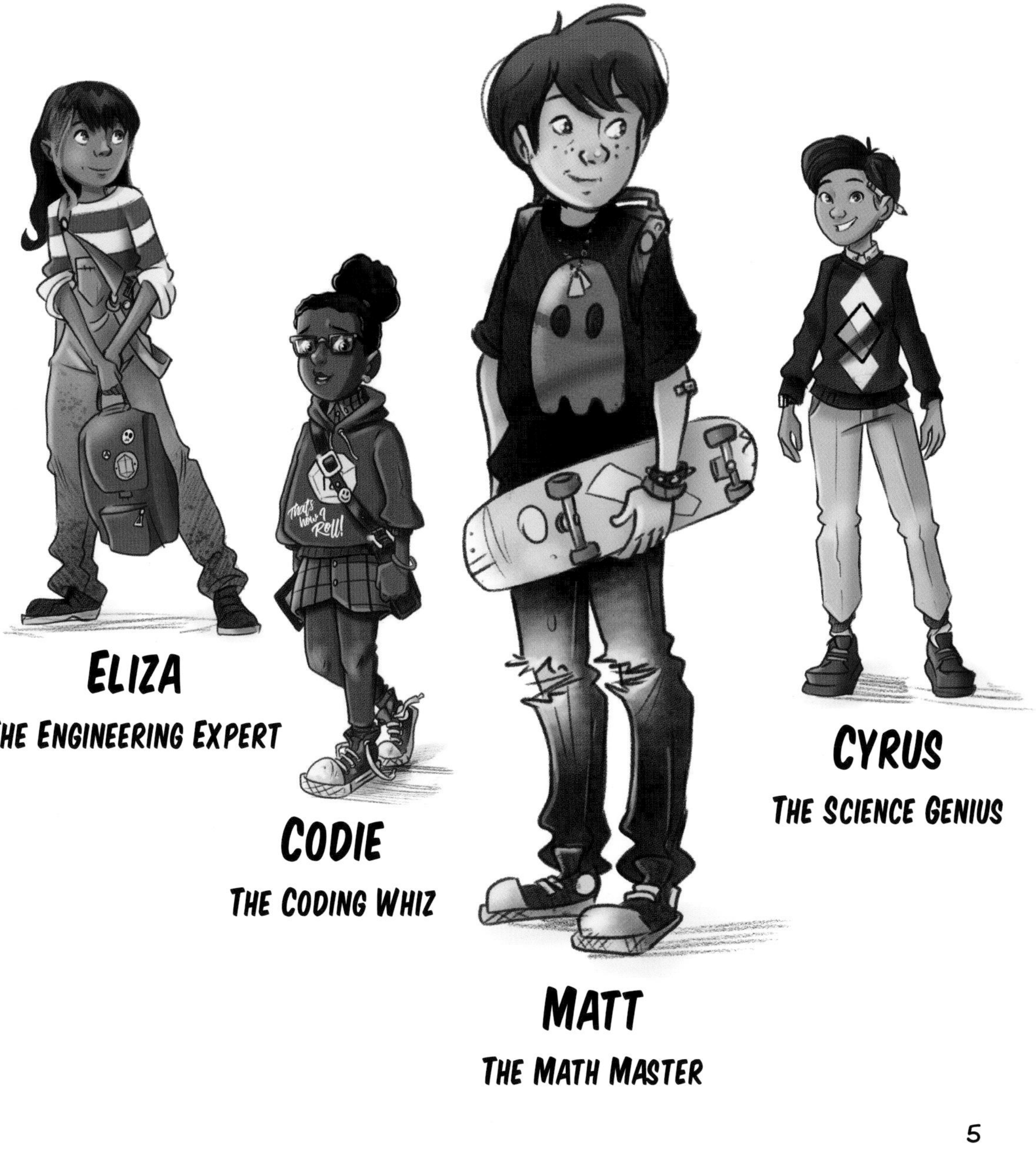
That's how I Roll!

ELIZA
THE ENGINEERING EXPERT

CODIE
THE CODING WHIZ

MATT
THE MATH MASTER

CYRUS
THE SCIENCE GENIUS

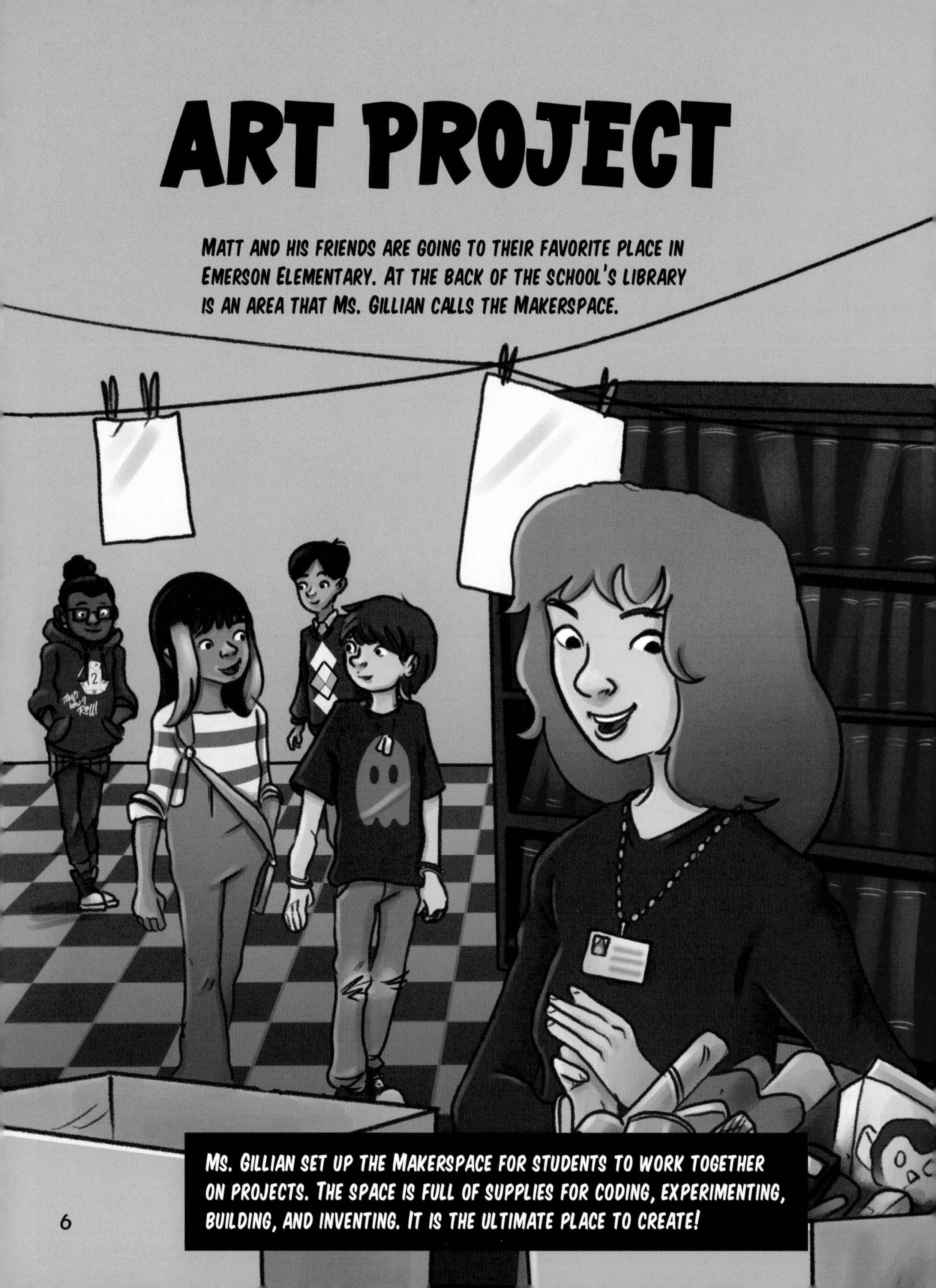
ART PROJECT
MATT AND HIS FRIENDS ARE GOING TO THEIR FAVORITE PLACE IN EMERSON ELEMENTARY. AT THE BACK OF THE SCHOOL'S LIBRARY IS AN AREA THAT MS. GILLIAN CALLS THE MAKERSPACE.
MS. GILLIAN SET UP THE MAKERSPACE FOR STUDENTS TO WORK TOGETHER ON PROJECTS. THE SPACE IS FULL OF SUPPLIES FOR CODING, EXPERIMENTING, BUILDING, AND INVENTING. IT IS THE ULTIMATE PLACE TO CREATE!

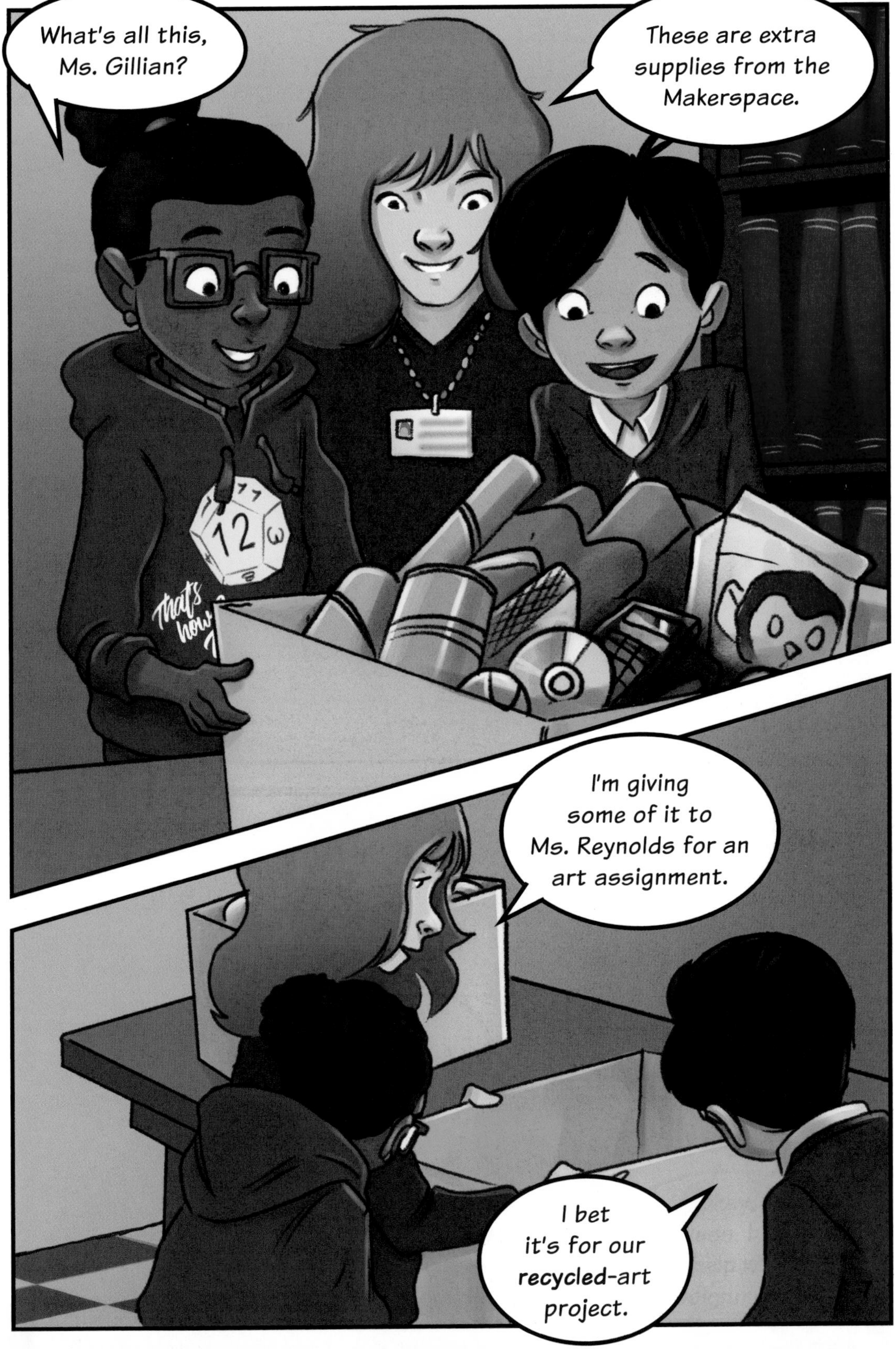
What's all this, Ms. Gillian?
These are extra supplies from the Makerspace.
I'm giving some of it to Ms. Reynolds for an art assignment.
I bet it's for our **recycled**-art project.

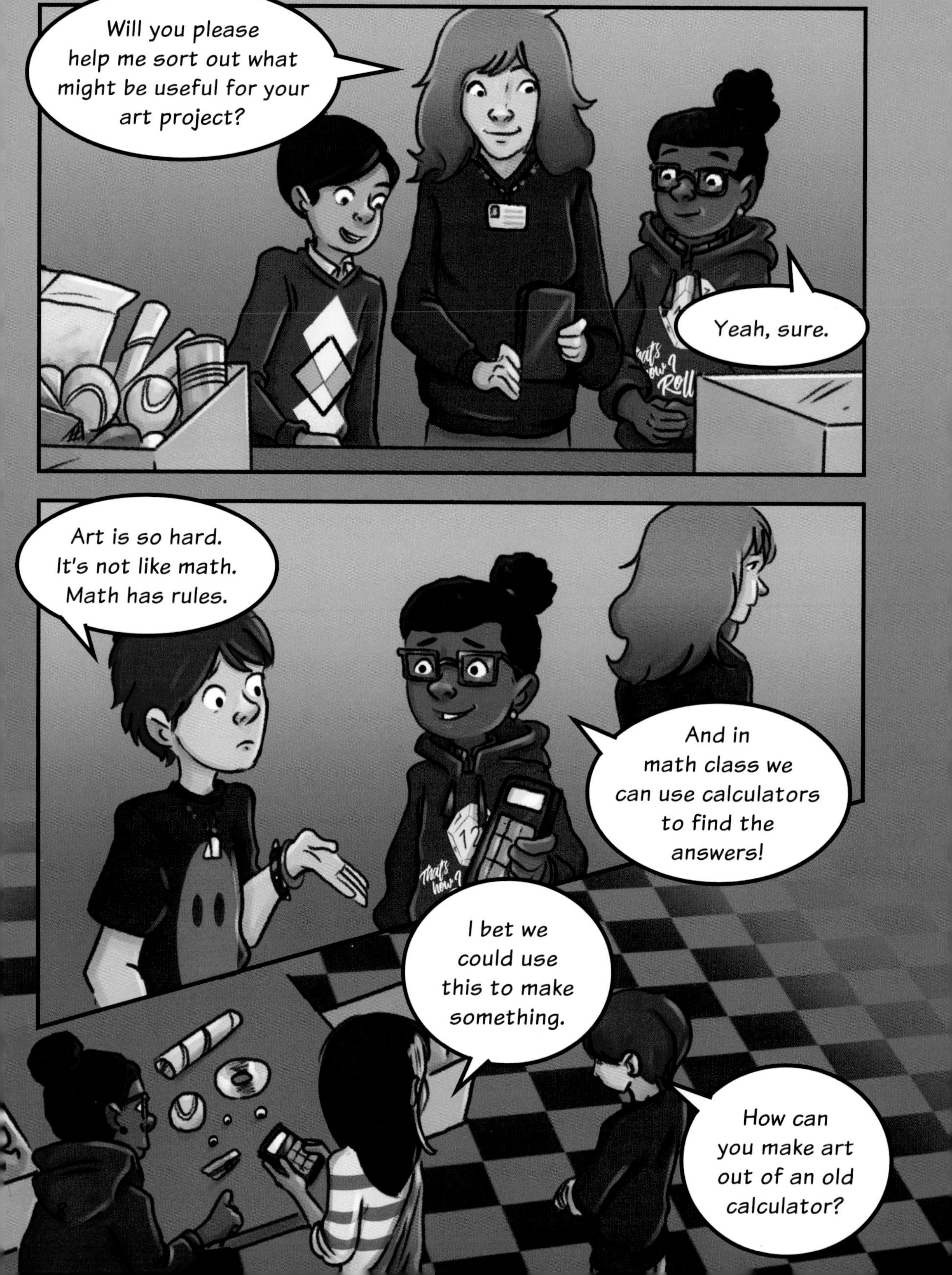
Will you please help me sort out what might be useful for your art project?
Yeah, sure.
Art is so hard. It's not like math. Math has rules.
And in math class we can use calculators to find the answers!
I bet we could use this to make something.
How can you make art out of an old calculator?

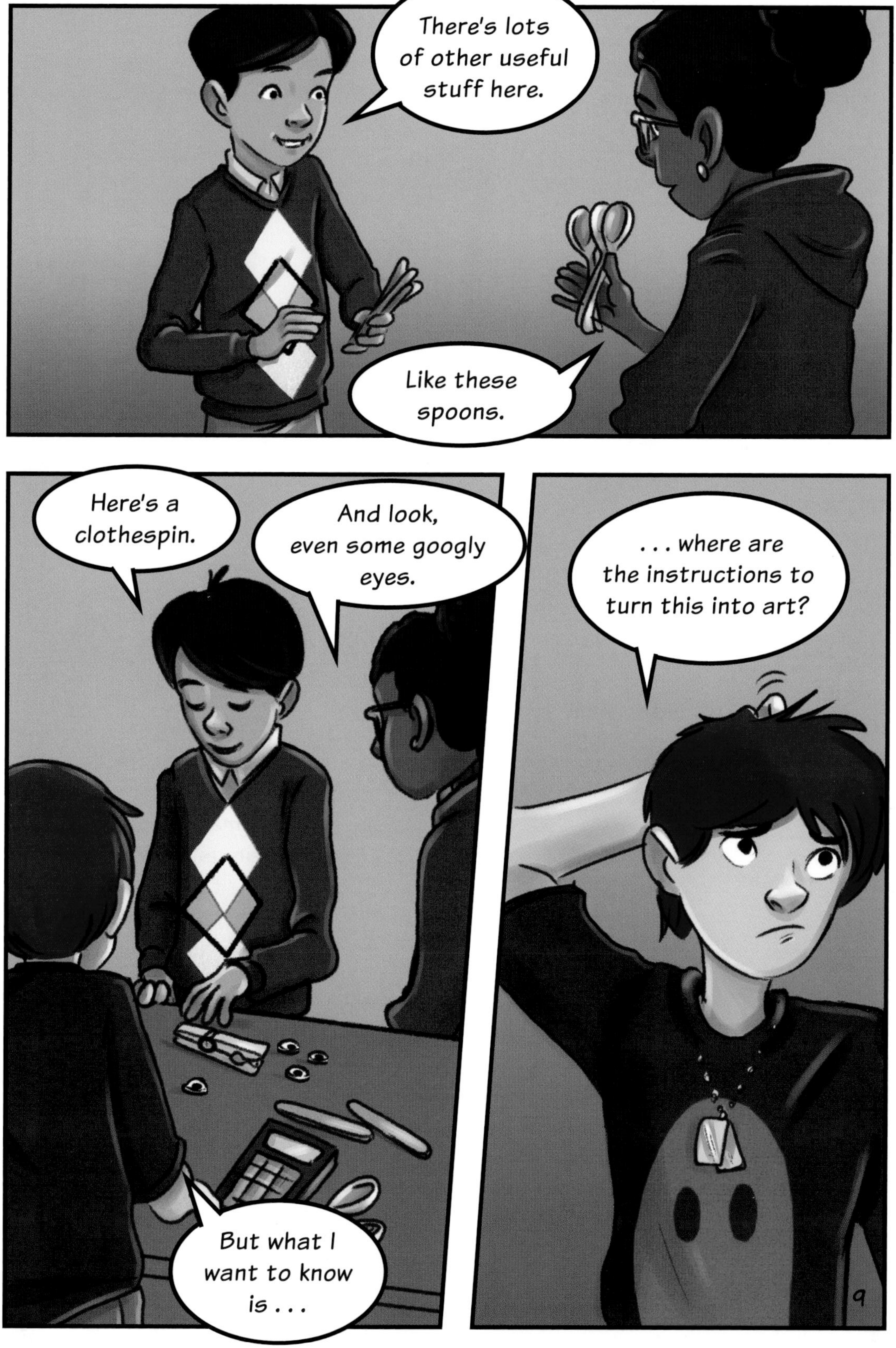
There's lots of other useful stuff here.
Like these spoons.
Here's a clothespin.
And look, even some googly eyes.
But what I want to know is . . .
. . . where are the instructions to turn this into art?

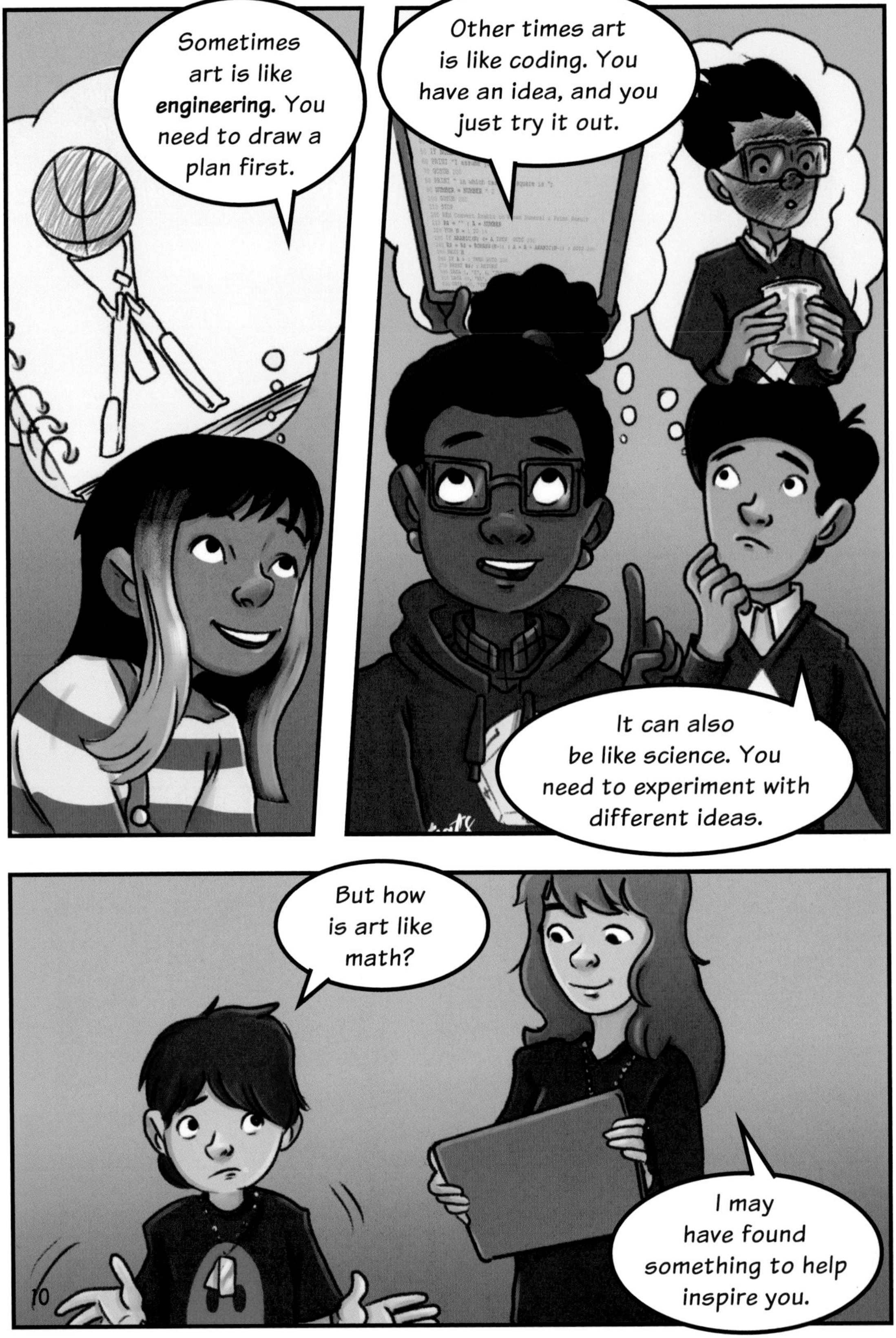

Sometimes art is like **engineering.** You need to draw a plan first.
Other times art is like coding. You have an idea, and you just try it out.
It can also be like science. You need to experiment with different ideas.
But how is art like math?
I may have found something to help inspire you.

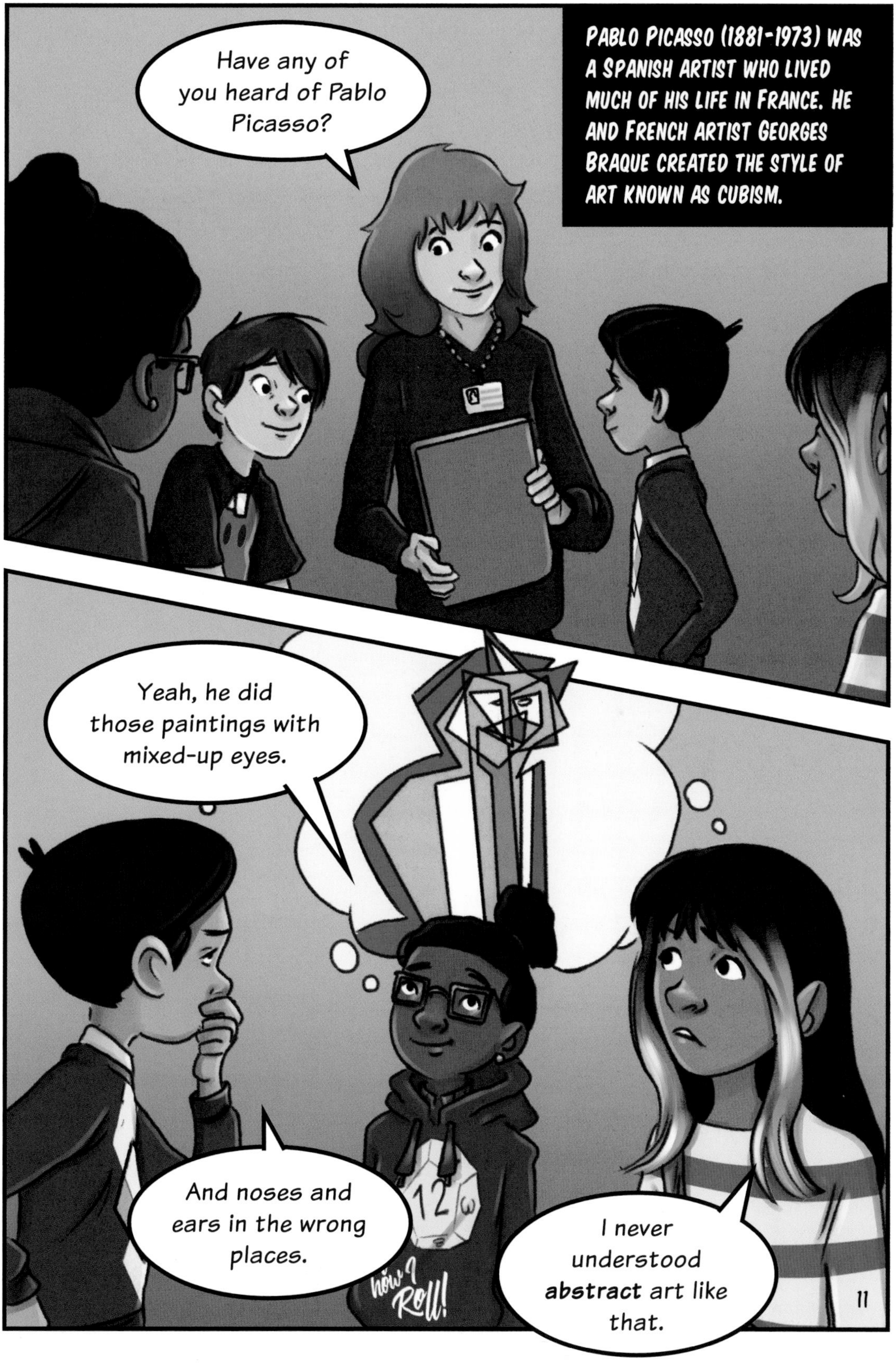

Have any of you heard of Pablo Picasso?
PABLO PICASSO (1881-1973) WAS A SPANISH ARTIST WHO LIVED MUCH OF HIS LIFE IN FRANCE. HE AND FRENCH ARTIST GEORGES BRAQUE CREATED THE STYLE OF ART KNOWN AS CUBISM.
Yeah, he did those paintings with mixed-up eyes.
And noses and ears in the wrong places.
I never understood **abstract** art like that.

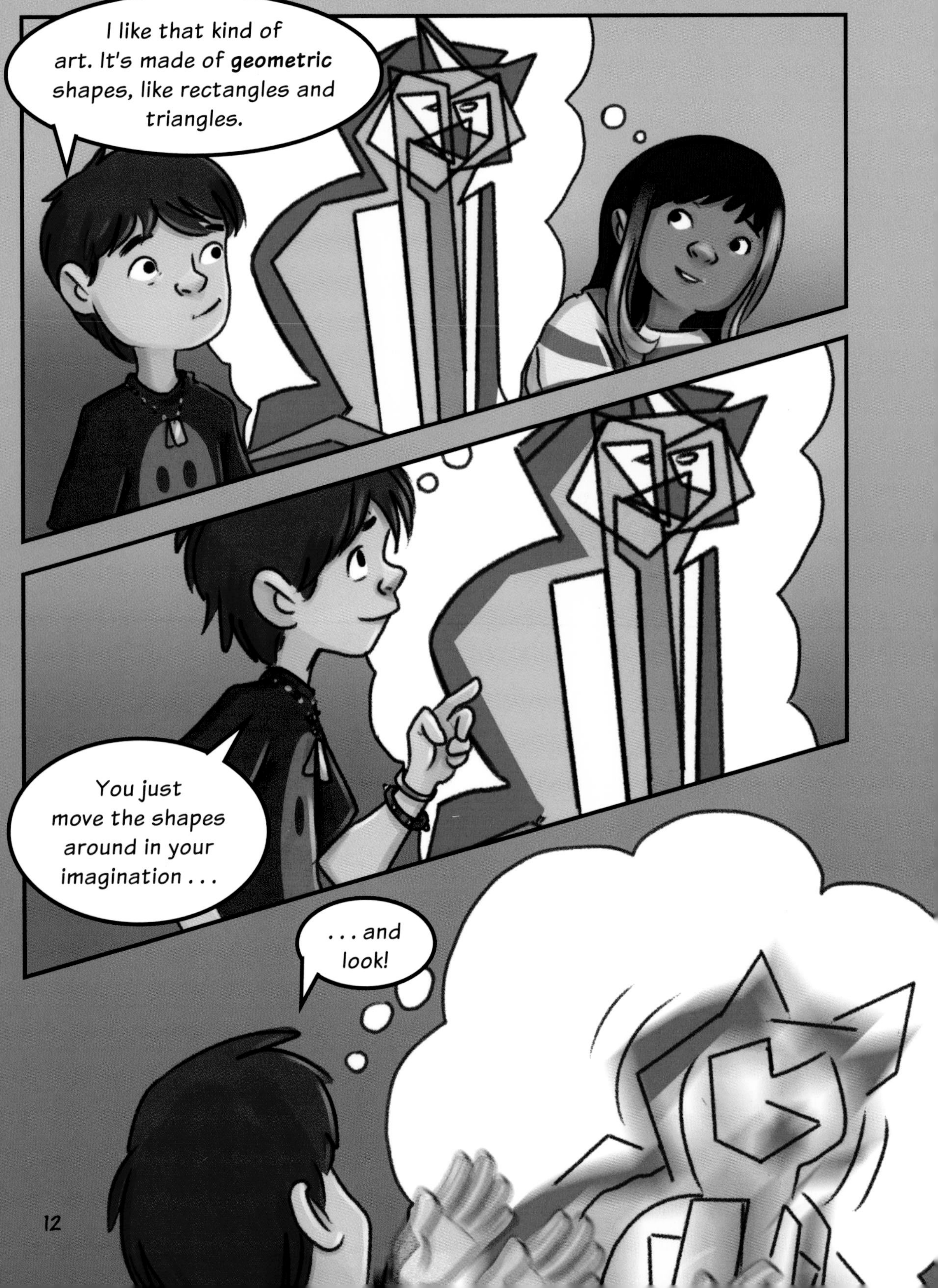
I like that kind of art. It's made of **geometric** shapes, like rectangles and triangles.
You just move the shapes around in your imagination . . .
. . . and look!

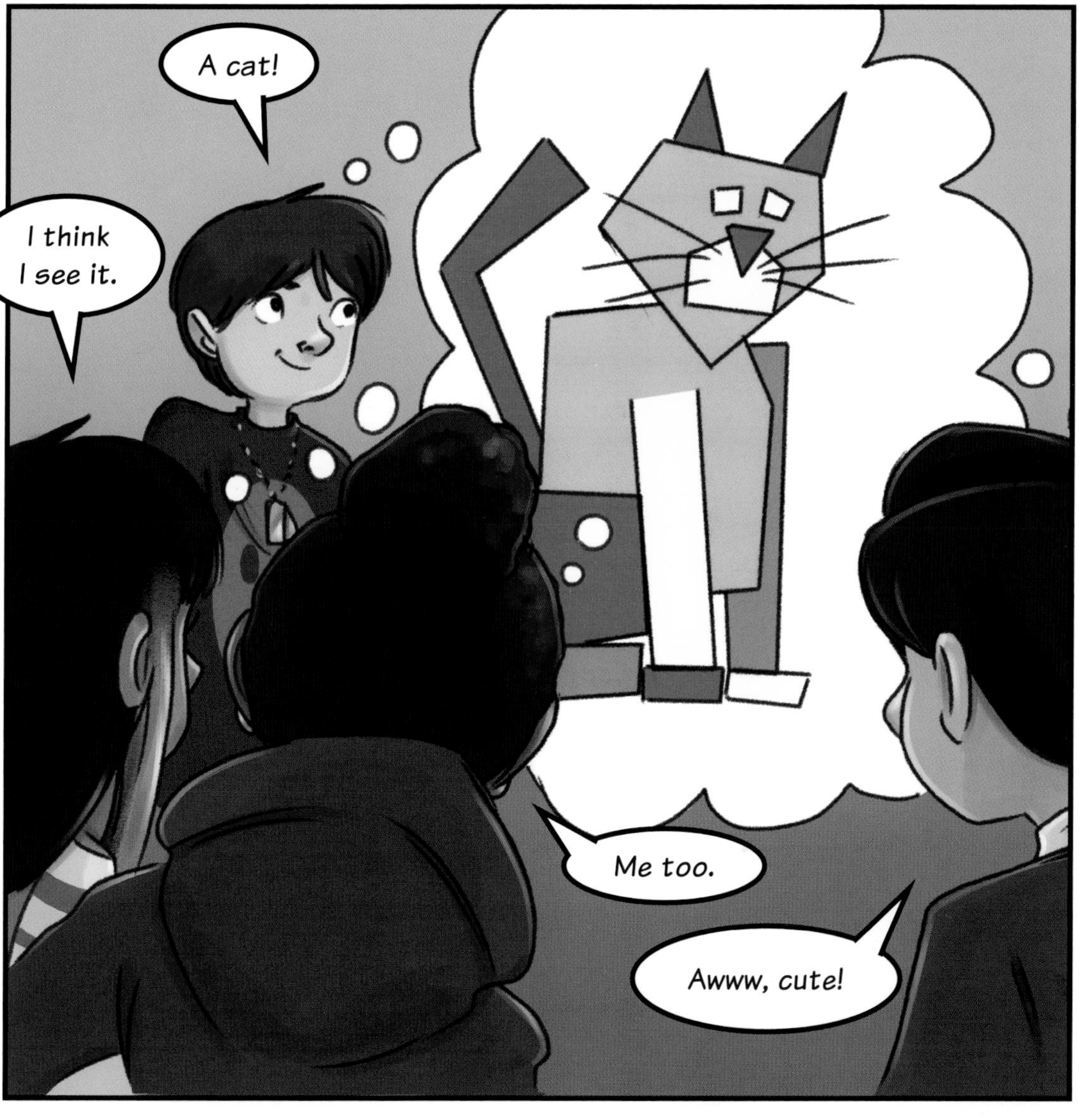
A cat!
I think I see it.
Me too.
Awww, cute!

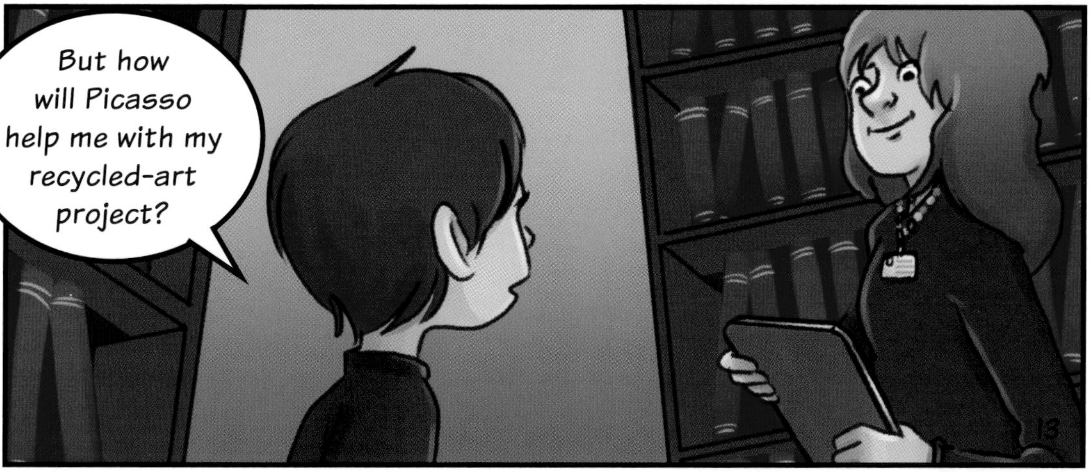
But how will Picasso help me with my recycled-art project?

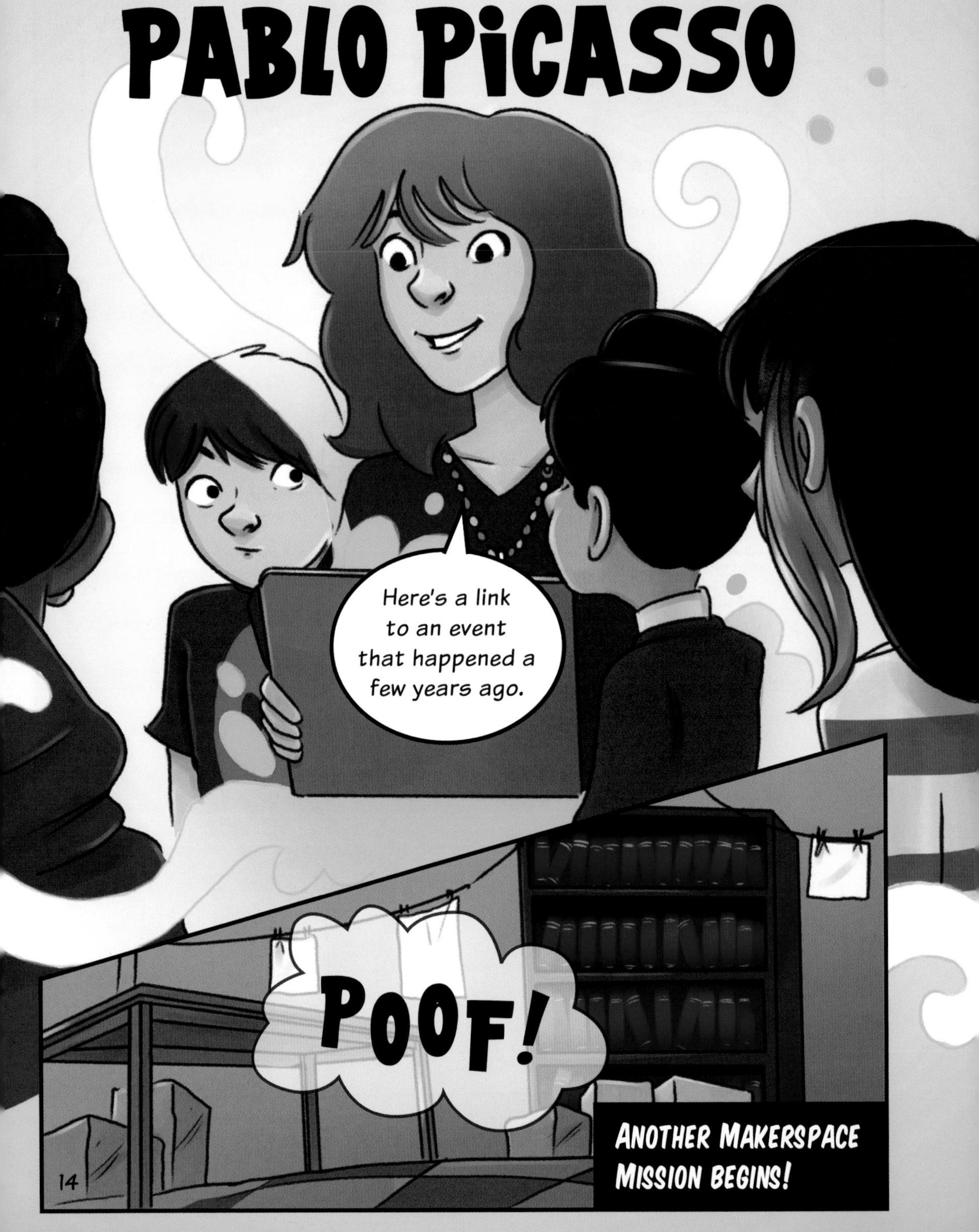
PABLO PICASSO
Here's a link to an event that happened a few years ago.
POOF!
ANOTHER MAKERSPACE MISSION BEGINS!

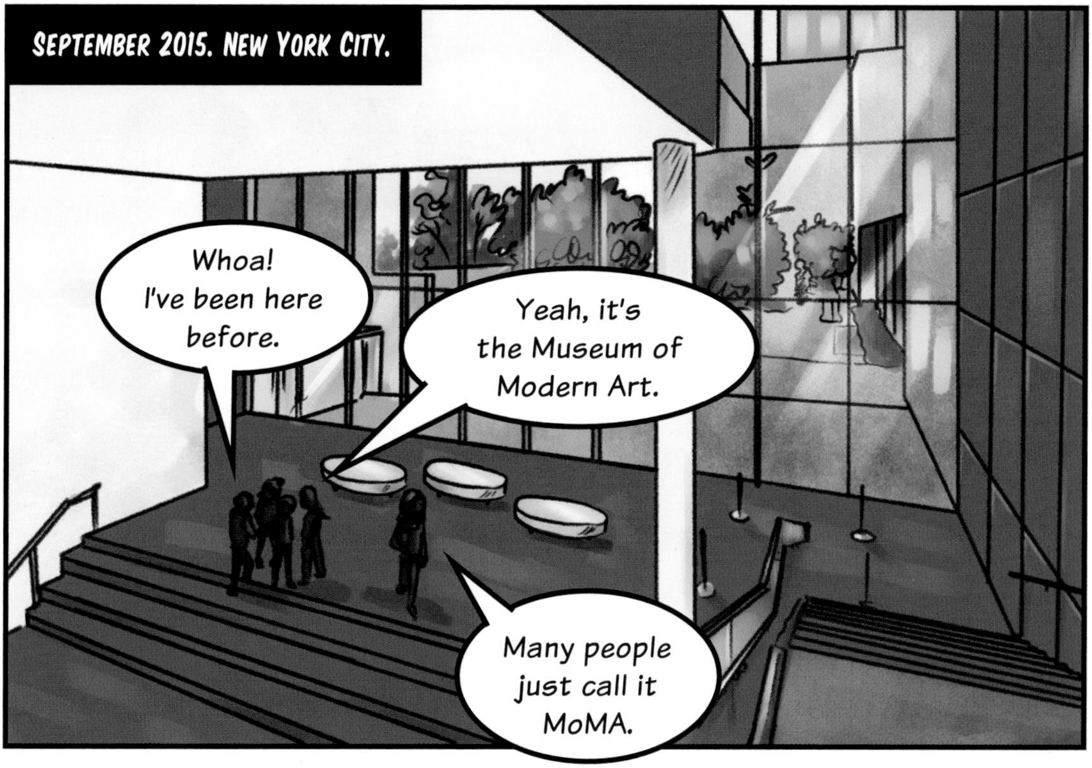
SEPTEMBER 2015. NEW YORK CITY.
Whoa! I've been here before.
Yeah, it's the Museum of Modern Art.
Many people just call it MoMA.

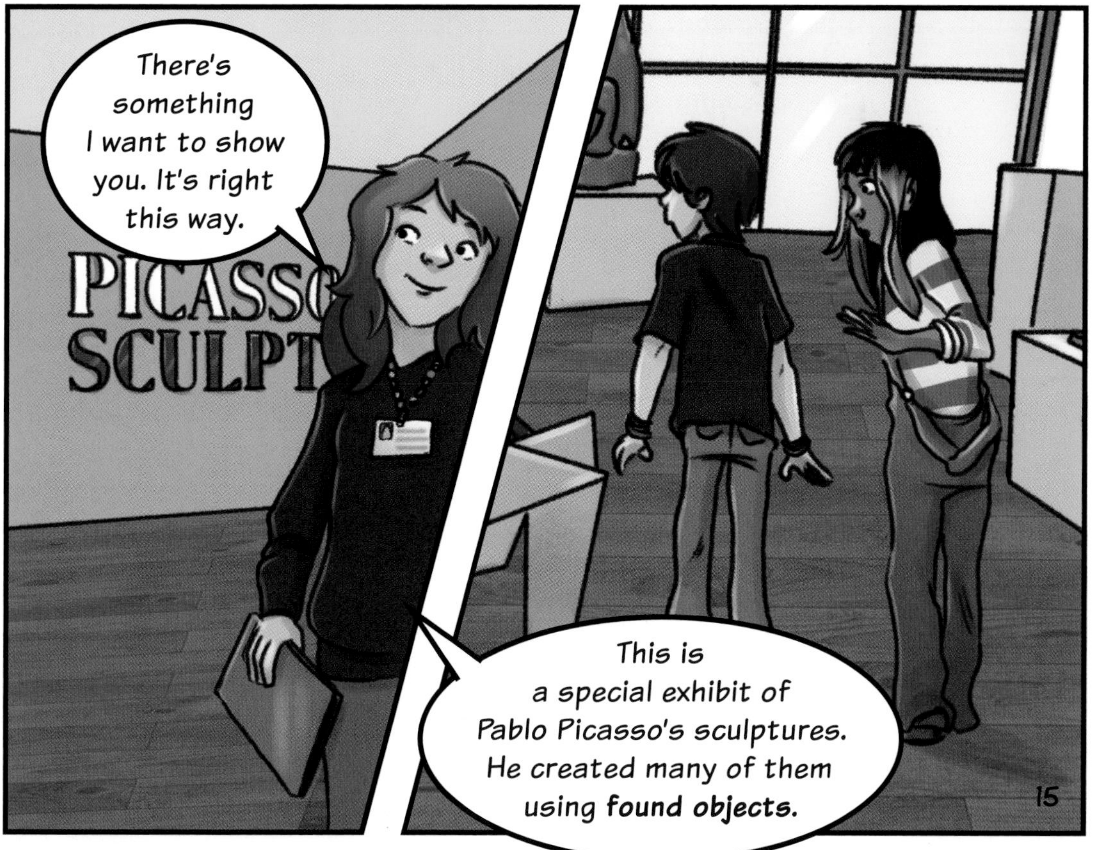
There's something I want to show you. It's right this way.
This is a special exhibit of Pablo Picasso's sculptures. He created many of them using found objects.

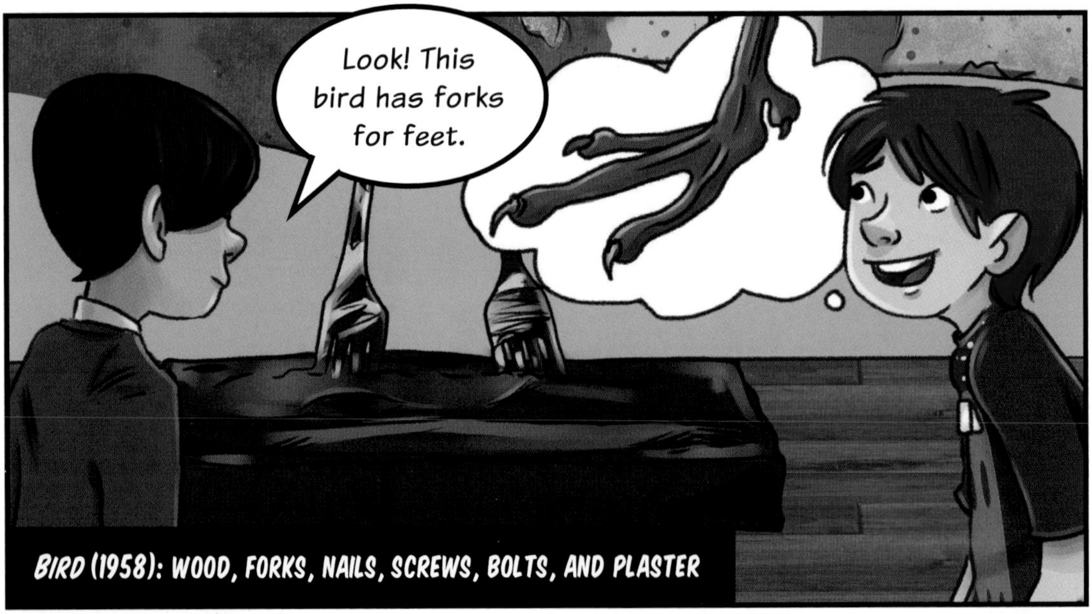
Look! This bird has forks for feet.

BIRD (1958): WOOD, FORKS, NAILS, SCREWS, BOLTS, AND PLASTER

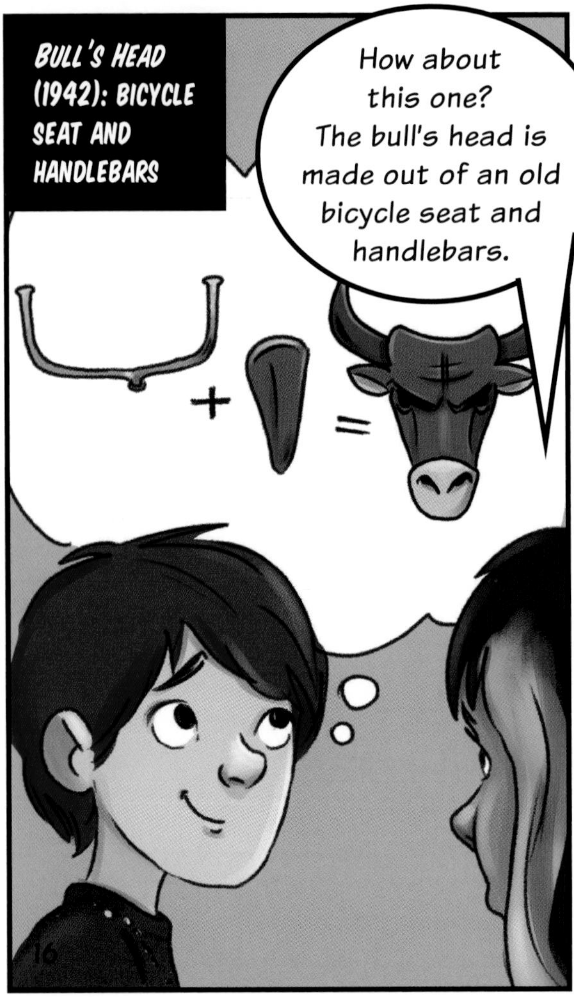
How about this one? The bull's head is made out of an old bicycle seat and handlebars.
+
=

BULL'S HEAD (1942): BICYCLE SEAT AND HANDLEBARS

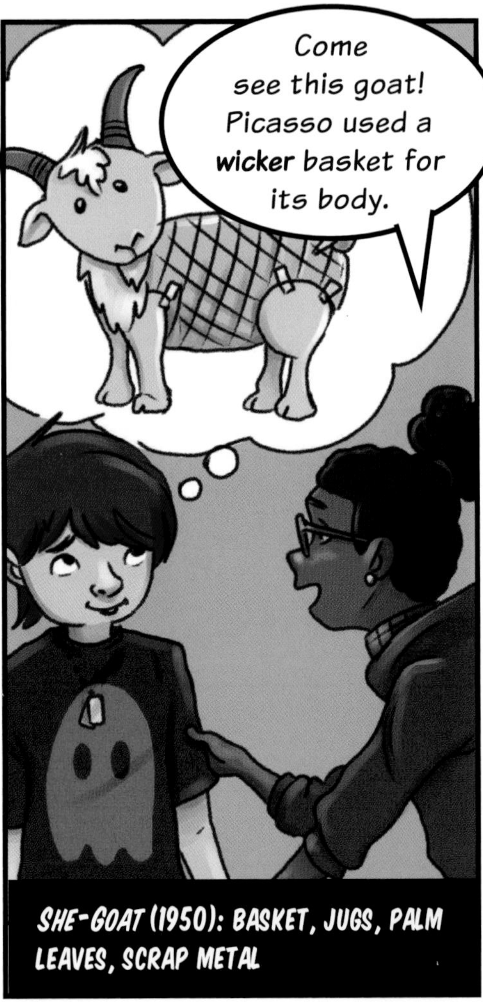
Come see this goat! Picasso used a **wicker** basket for its body.

SHE-GOAT (1950): BASKET, JUGS, PALM LEAVES, SCRAP METAL

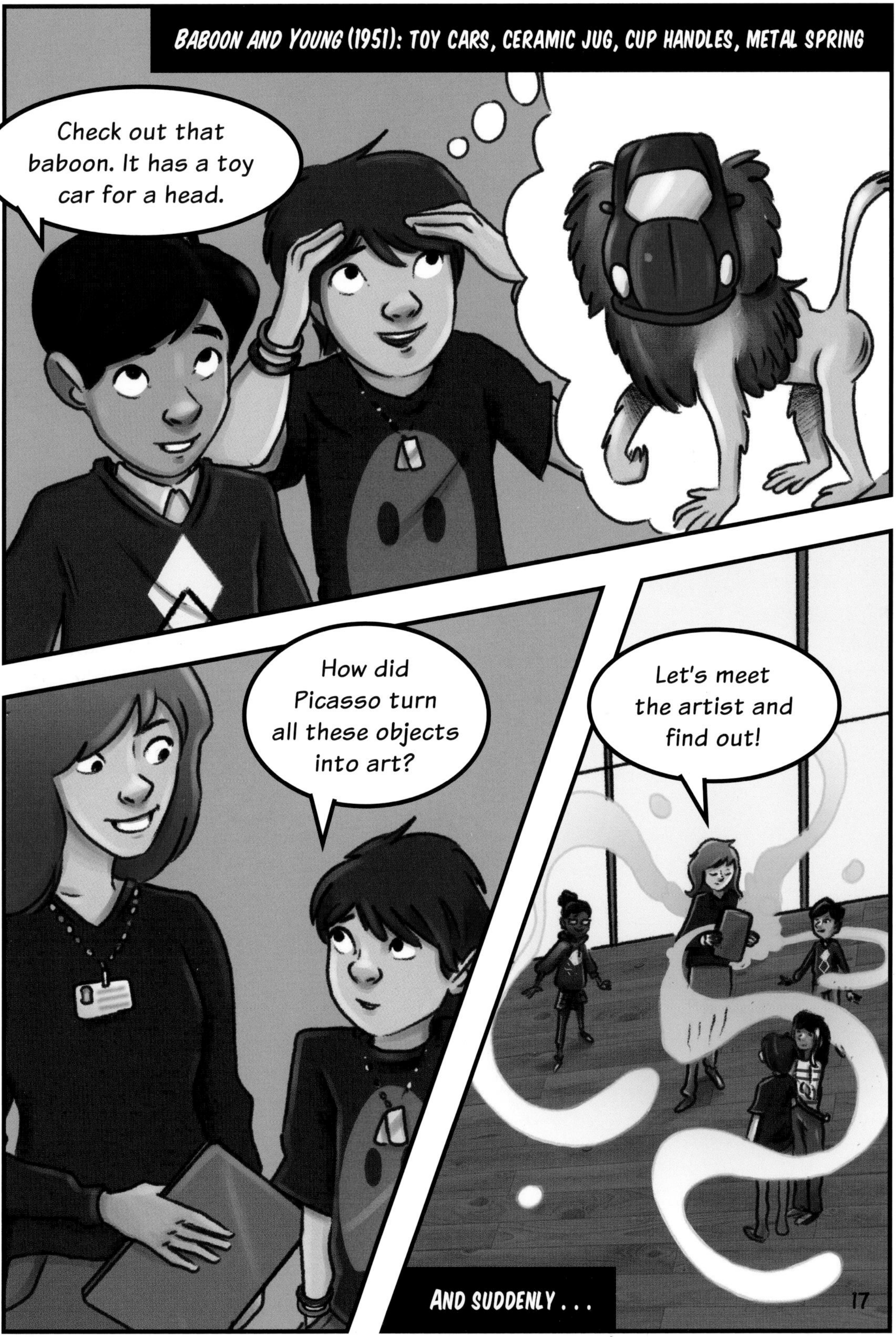
BABOON AND YOUNG (1951): TOY CARS, CERAMIC JUG, CUP HANDLES, METAL SPRING
Check out that baboon. It has a toy car for a head.
How did Picasso turn all these objects into art?
Let's meet the artist and find out!
AND SUDDENLY . . .

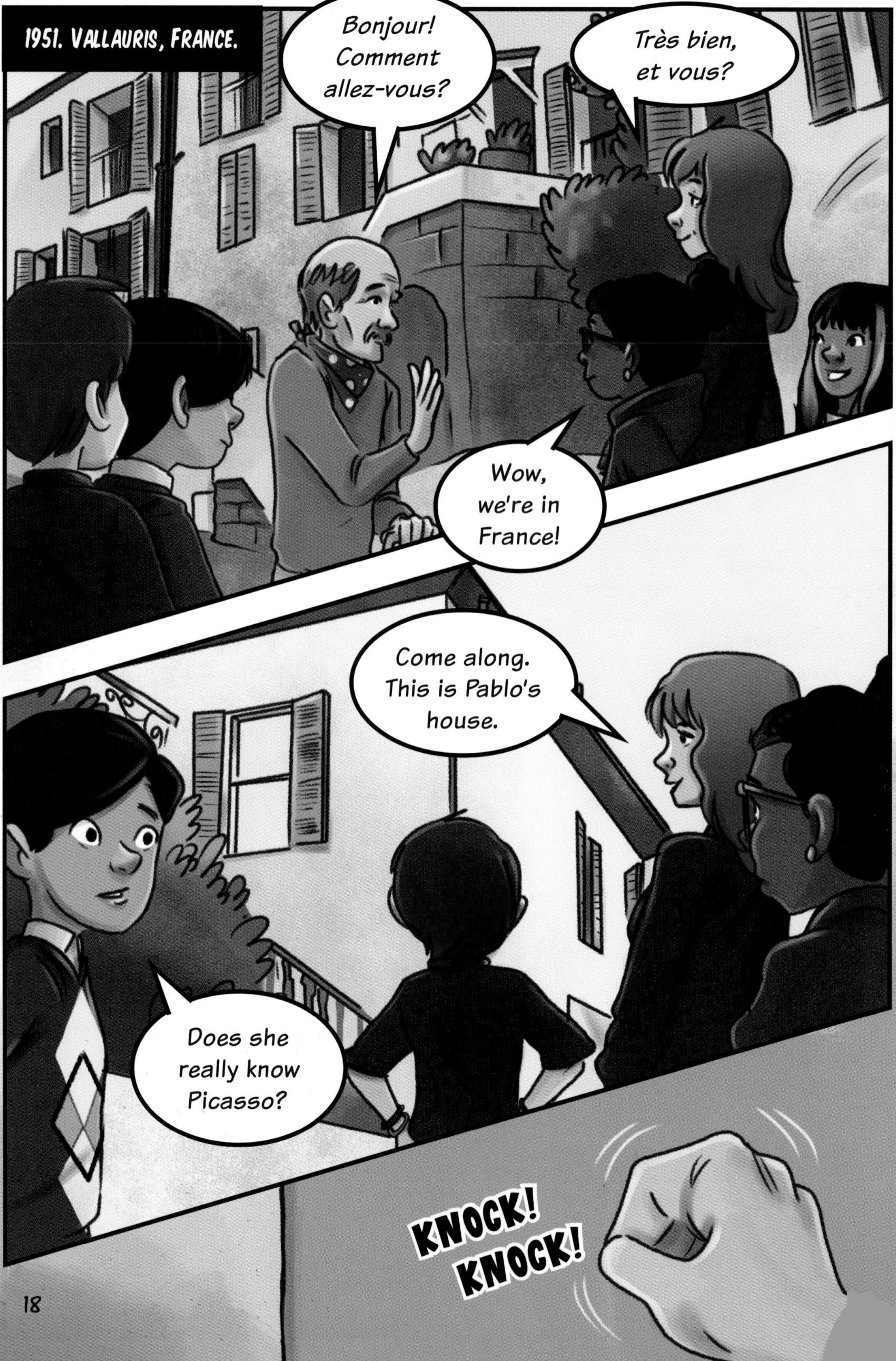
1951. VALLAURIS, FRANCE.
Bonjour! Comment allez-vous?
Très bien, et vous?
Wow, we're in France!
Come along. This is Pablo's house.
Does she really know Picasso?
KNOCK! KNOCK!

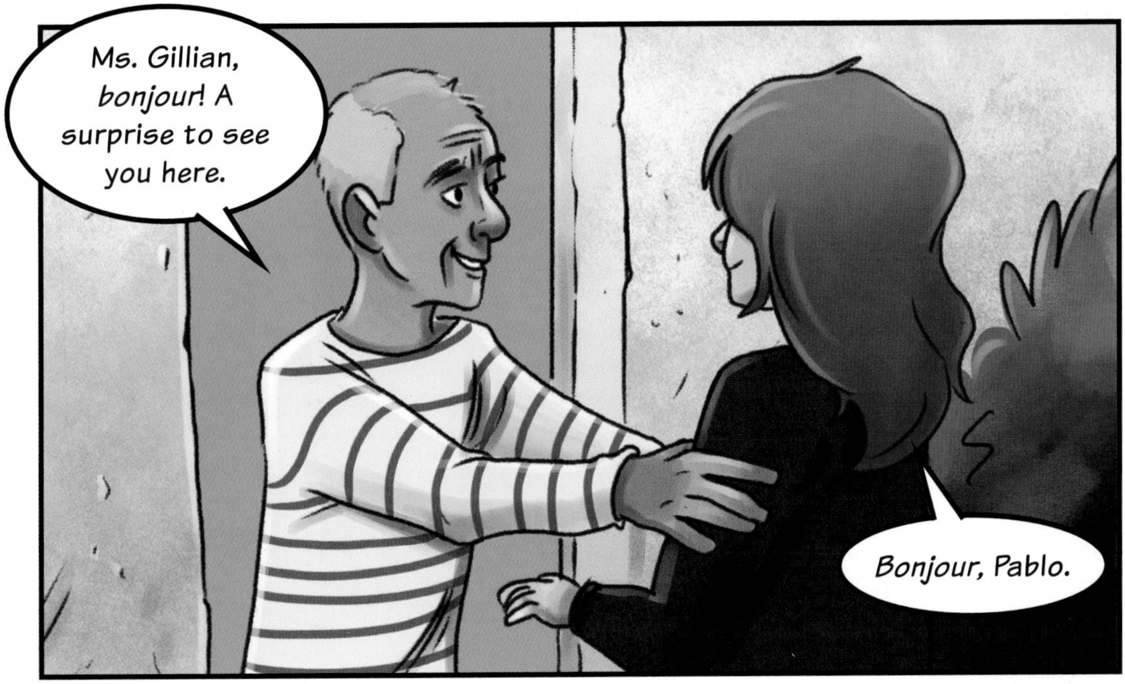
Ms. Gillian, *bonjour*! A surprise to see you here.
Bonjour, Pablo.

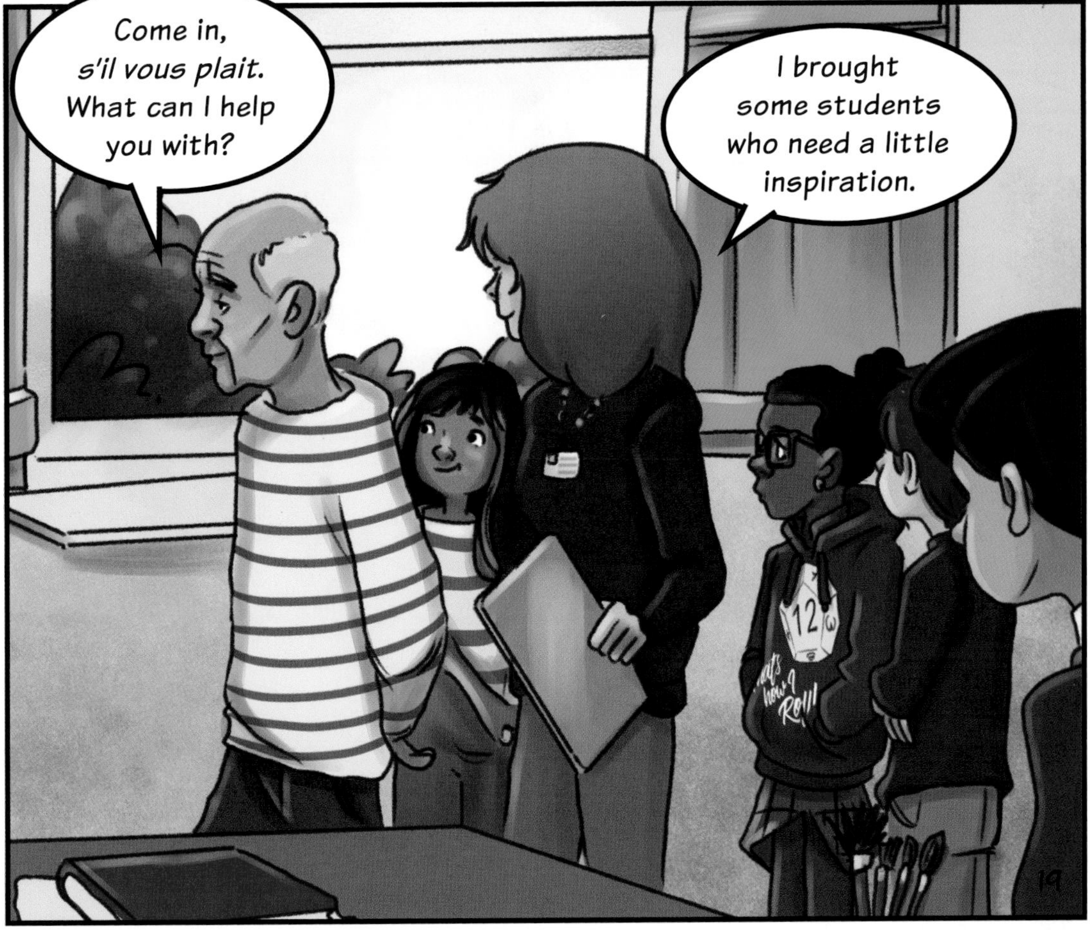
Come in, *s'il vous plait*. What can I help you with?
I brought some students who need a little inspiration.
12
That's how I Roll!

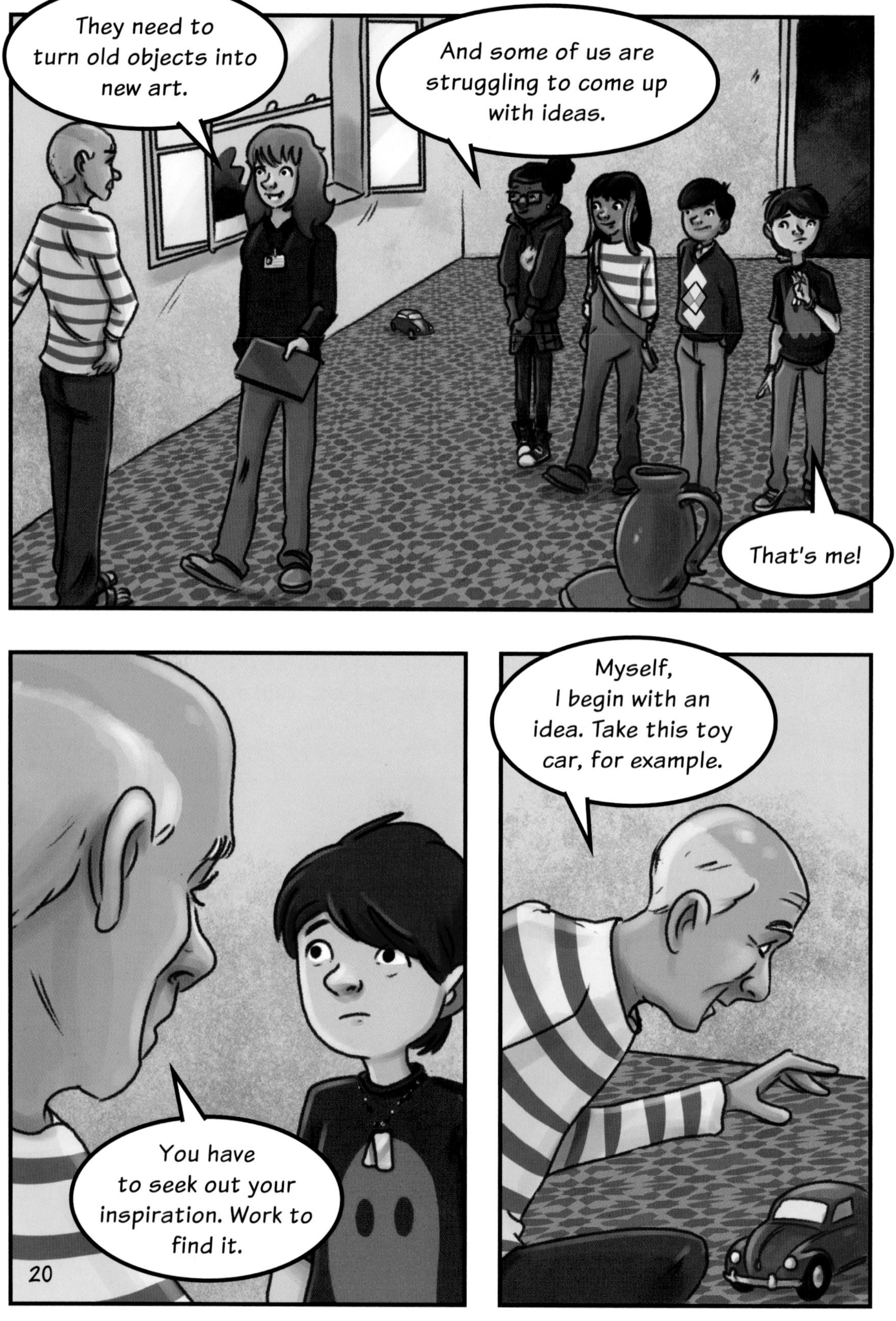
They need to turn old objects into new art.
And some of us are struggling to come up with ideas.
That's me!
You have to seek out your inspiration. Work to find it.
Myself, I begin with an idea. Take this toy car, for example.

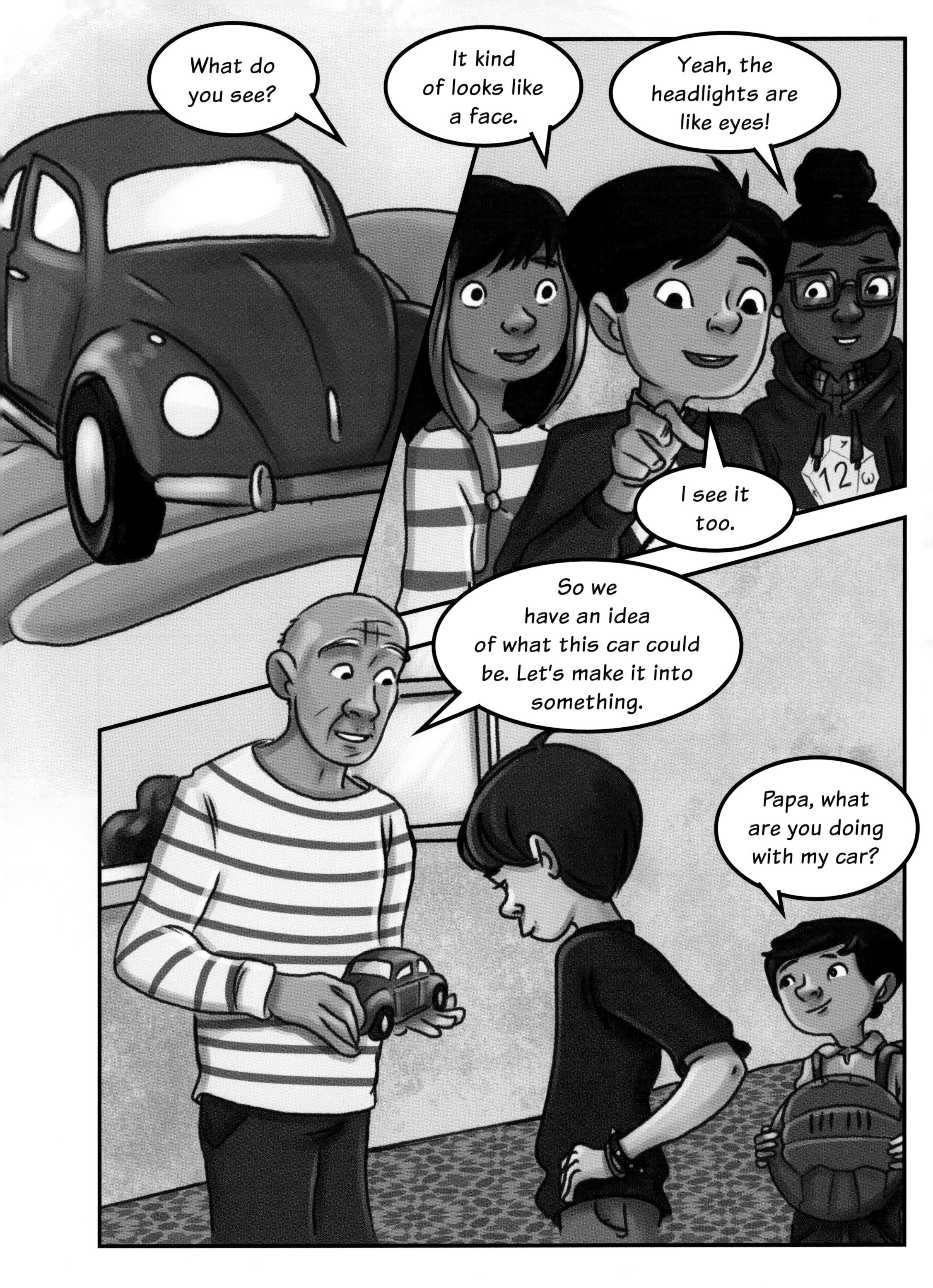
What do you see?
It kind of looks like a face.
Yeah, the headlights are like eyes!
I see it too.
So we have an idea of what this car could be. Let's make it into something.
Papa, what are you doing with my car?

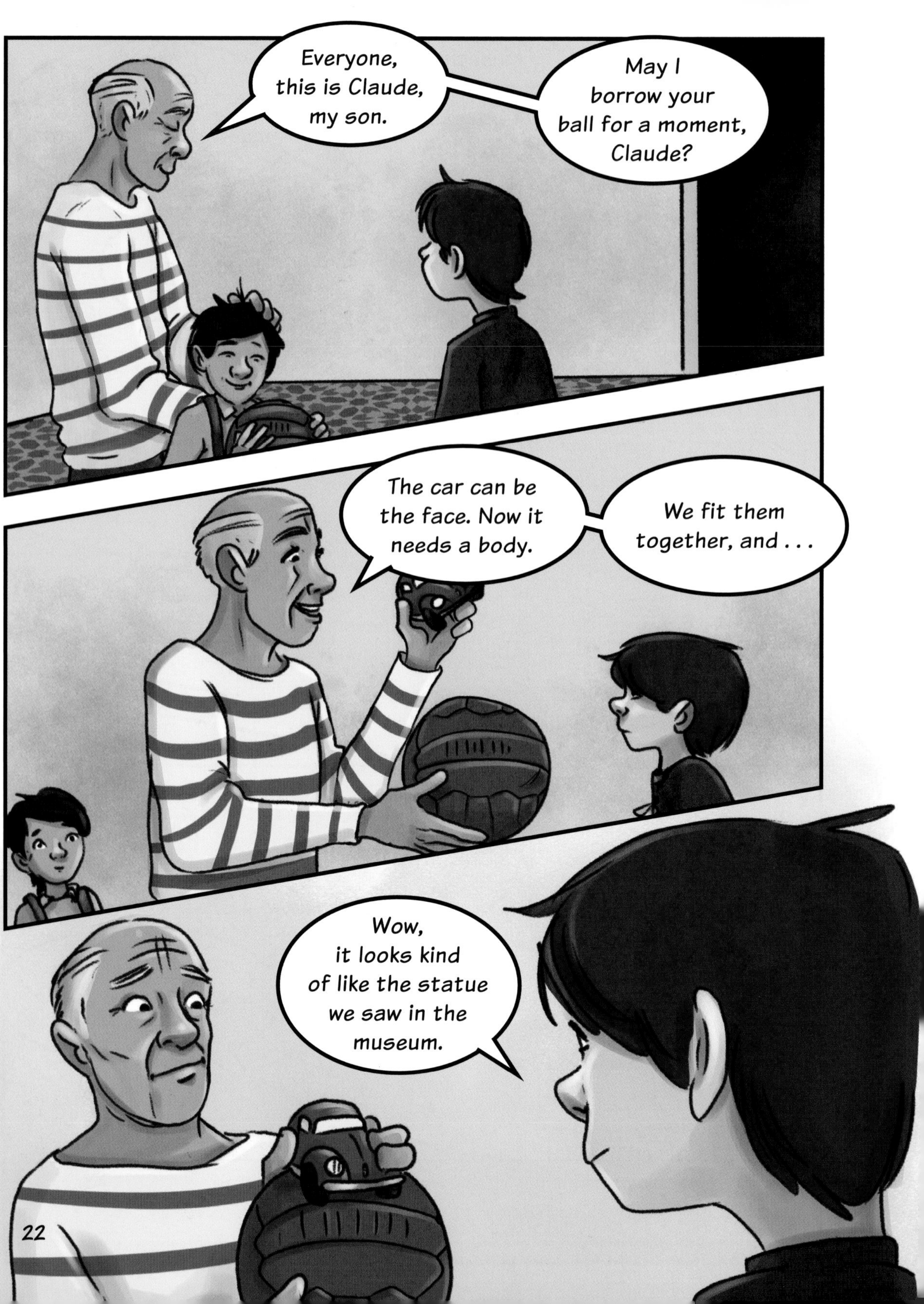
Everyone, this is Claude, my son.
May I borrow your ball for a moment, Claude?
The car can be the face. Now it needs a body.
We fit them together, and . . .
Wow, it looks kind of like the statue we saw in the museum.

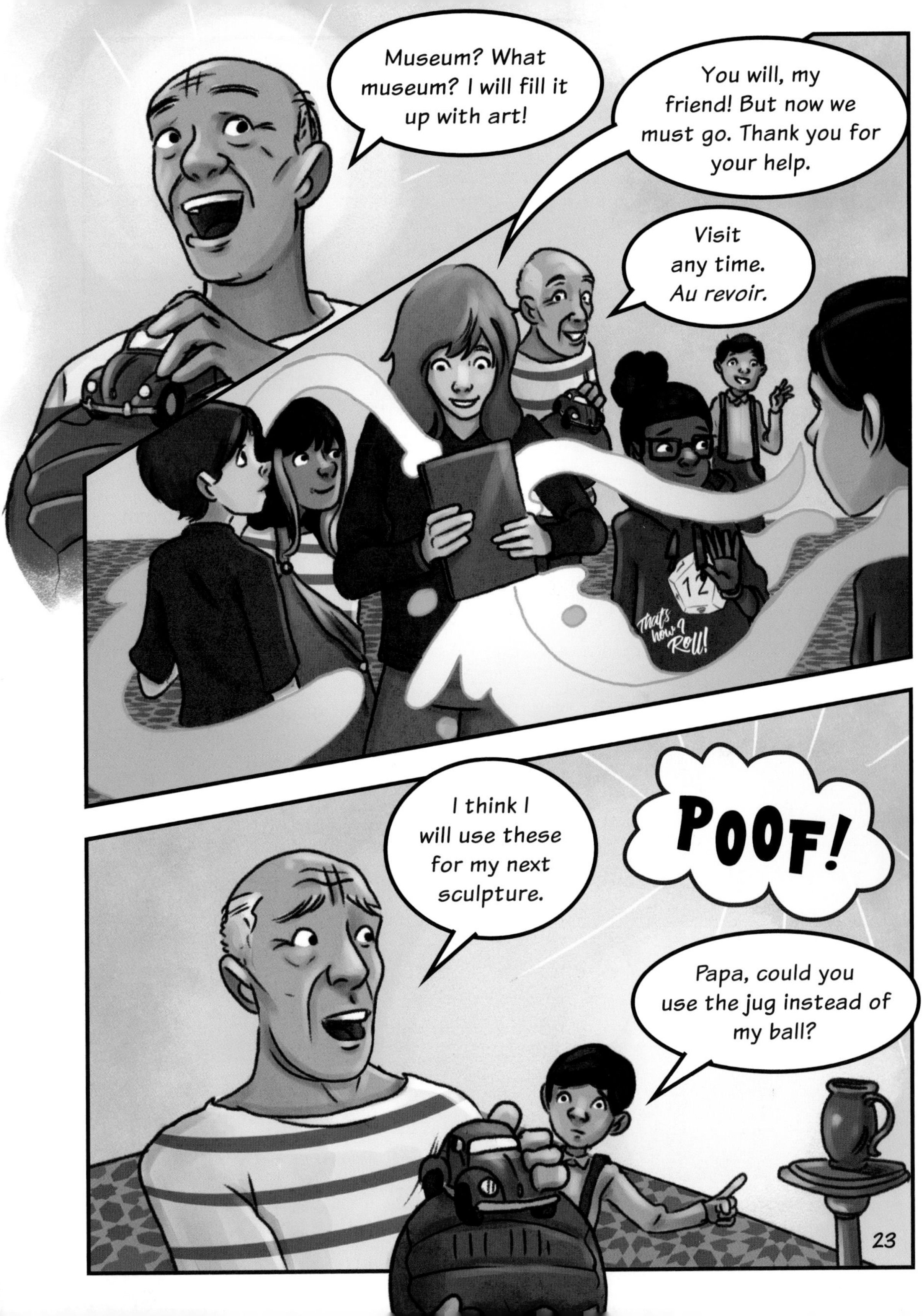
Museum? What museum? I will fill it up with art!
You will, my friend! But now we must go. Thank you for your help.
Visit any time. Au revoir.
That's how I Roll!
I think I will use these for my next sculpture.
POOF!
Papa, could you use the jug instead of my ball?

CRITTER ART

Wow! I can't believe we met Picasso.
Now I'm excited about our recycled-art project.
That's how I ROLL!
Let's make animal sculptures like Picasso!

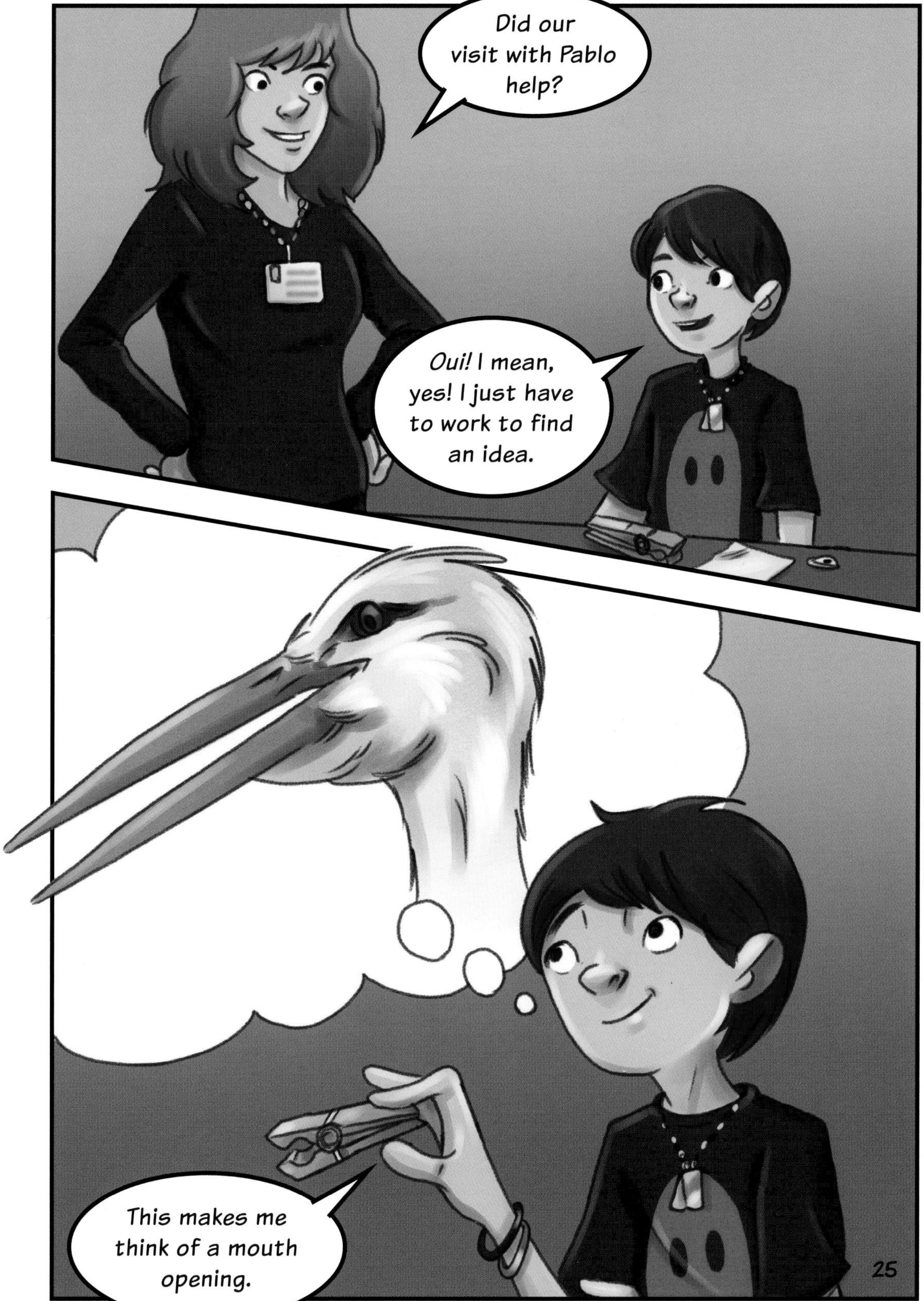
Did our visit with Pablo help?
Oui! I mean, yes! I just have to work to find an idea.
This makes me think of a mouth opening.

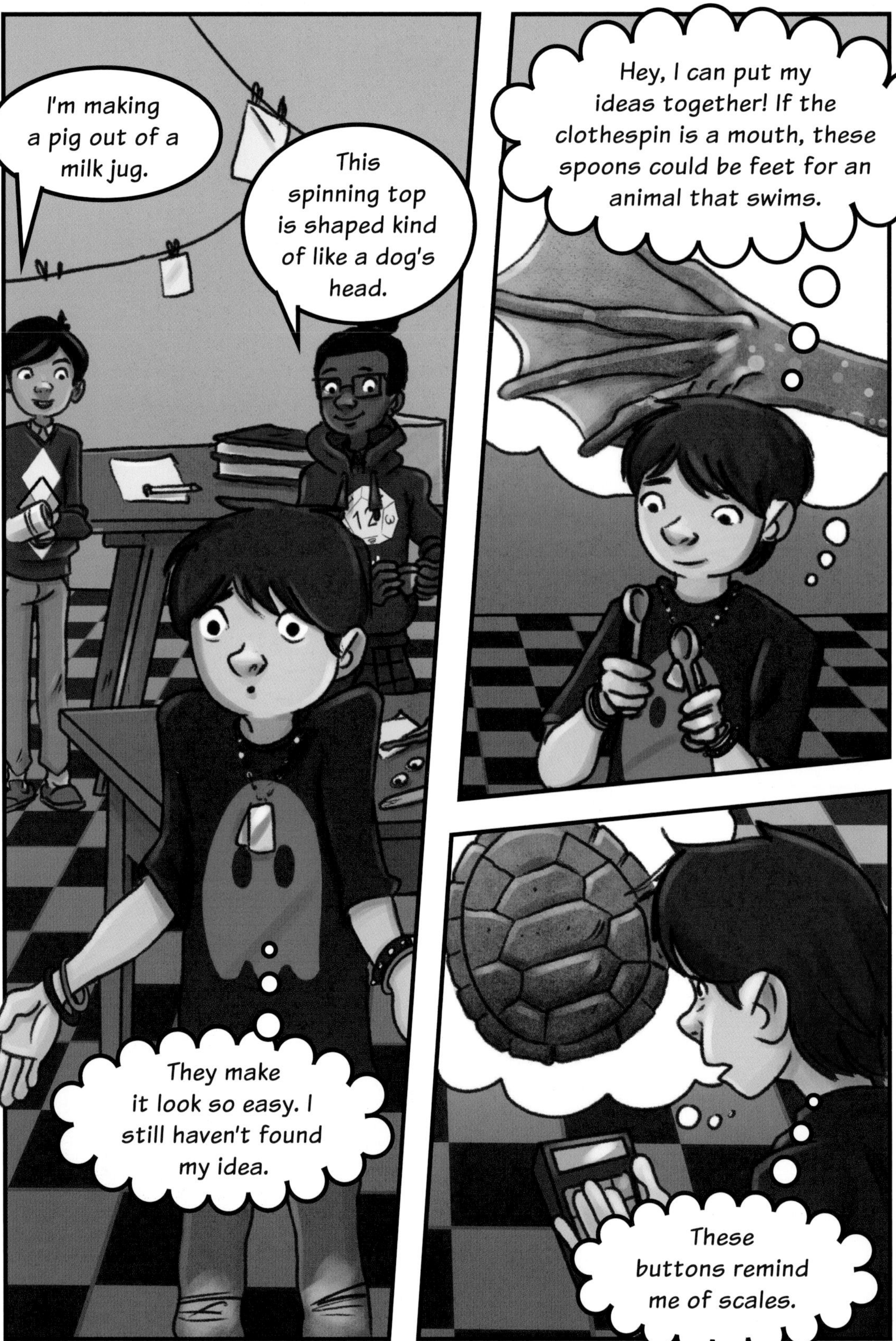
I'm making a pig out of a milk jug.
This spinning top is shaped kind of like a dog's head.
They make it look so easy. I still haven't found my idea.
Hey, I can put my ideas together! If the clothespin is a mouth, these spoons could be feet for an animal that swims.
These buttons remind me of scales.

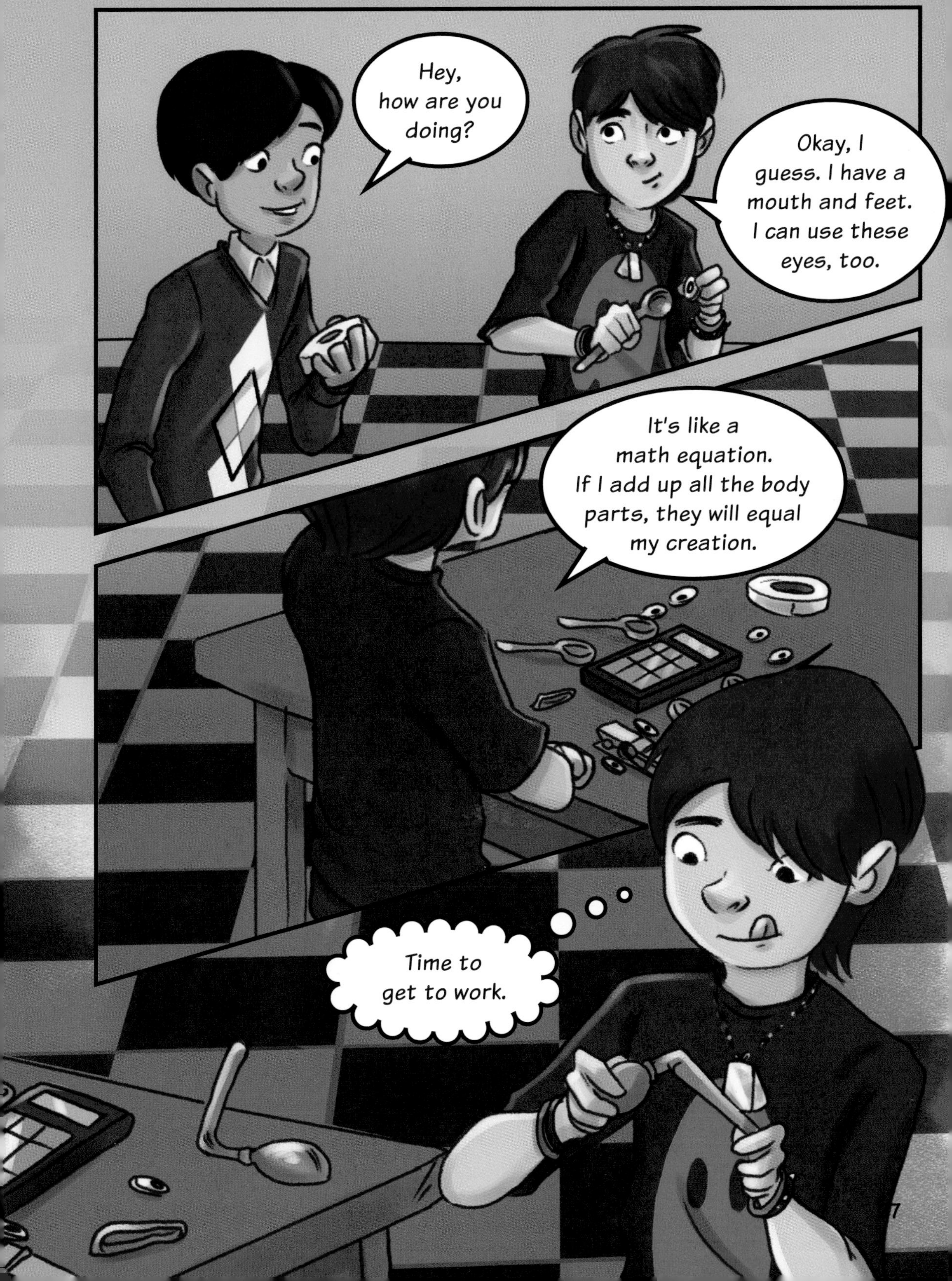
Hey, how are you doing?
Okay, I guess. I have a mouth and feet. I can use these eyes, too.
It's like a math equation. If I add up all the body parts, they will equal my creation.
Time to get to work.

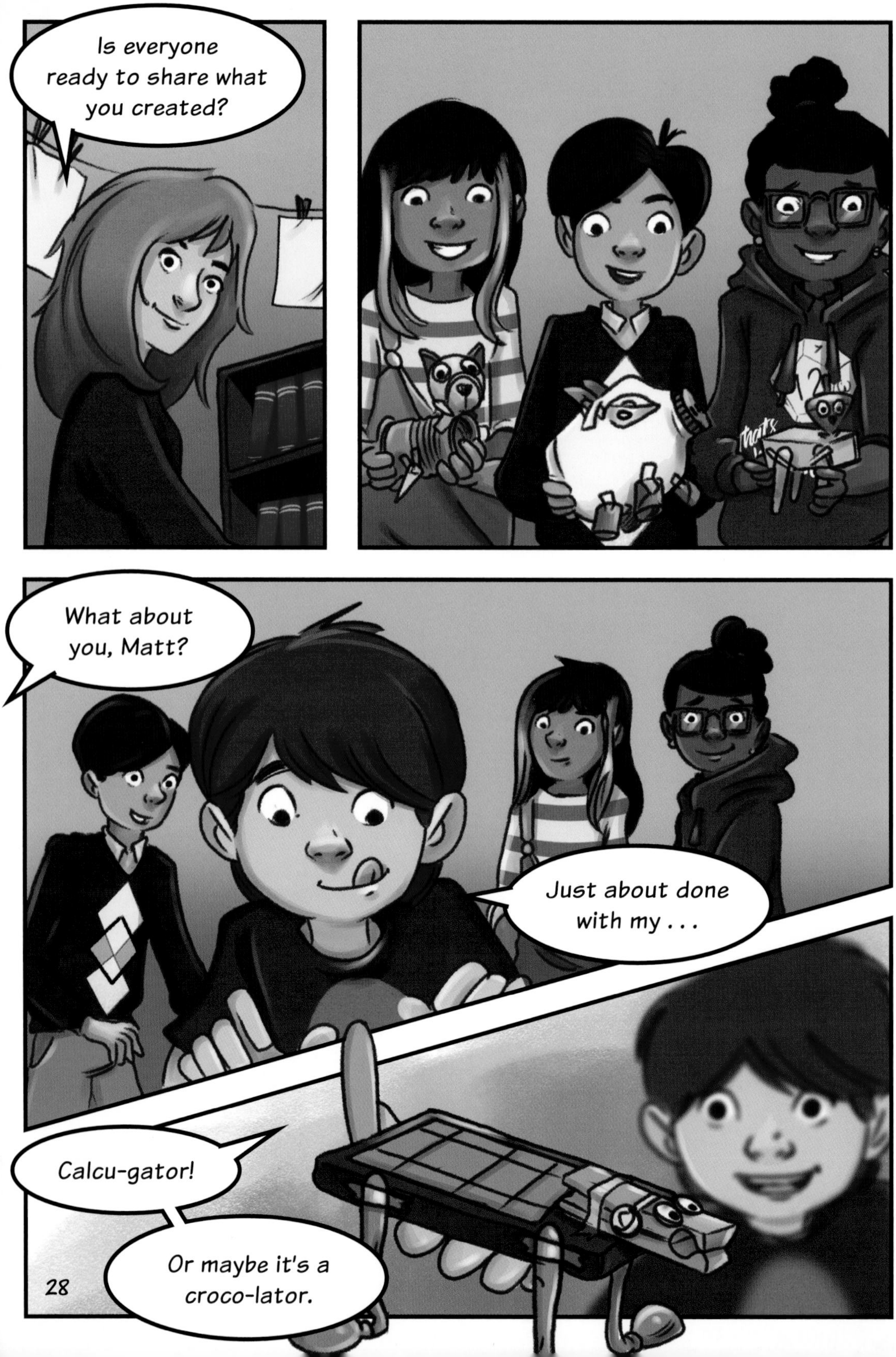

Is everyone ready to share what you created?
What about you, Matt?
Just about done with my . . .
Calcu-gator!
Or maybe it's a croco-lator.

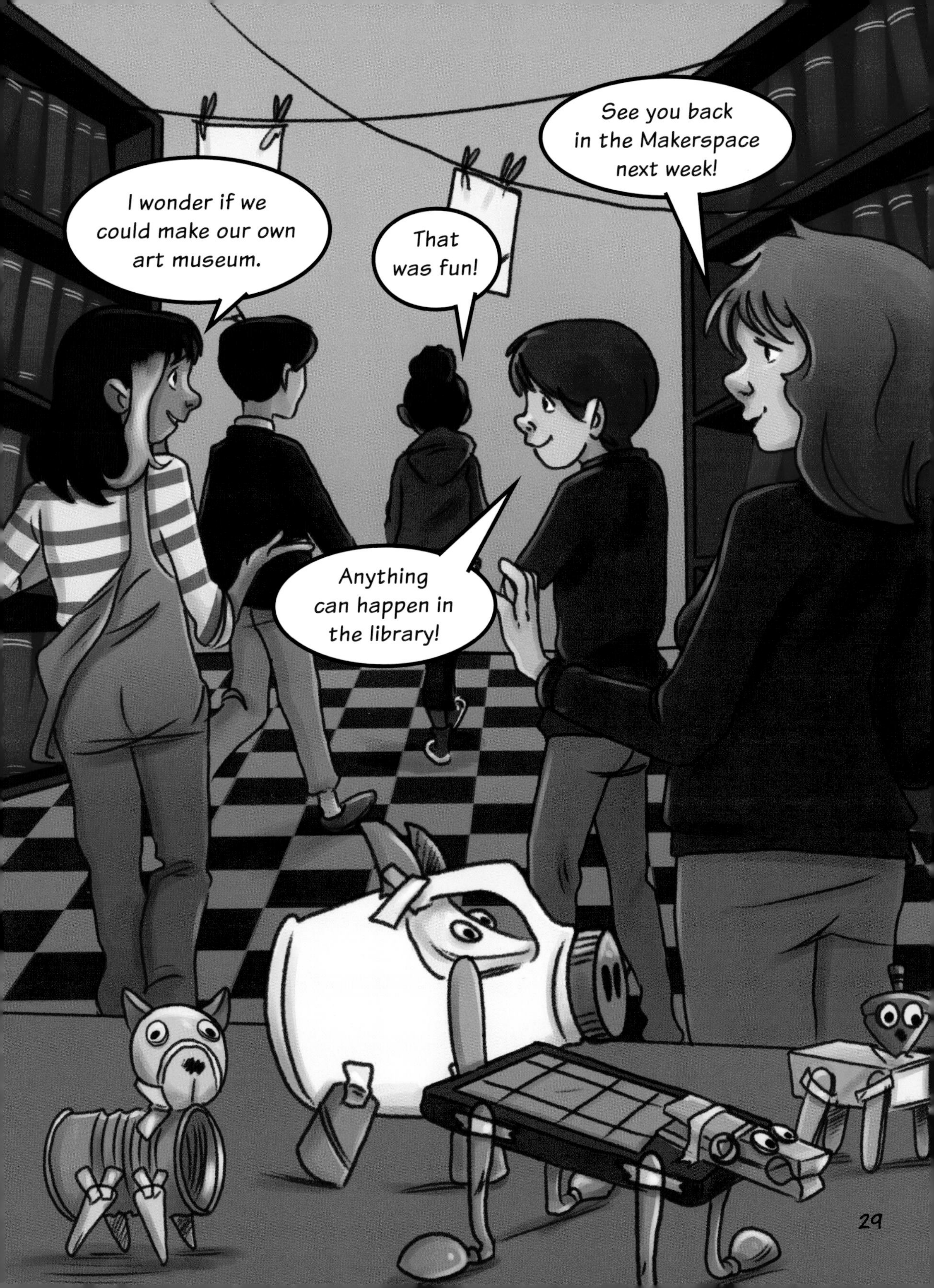

I wonder if we could make our own art museum.
That was fun!
See you back in the Makerspace next week!
Anything can happen in the library!

GLOSSARY

abstract—not realistic, as in abstract art

engineering—planning and building something

found objects—items that are either thrown away, such as bottles and cans, or discovered in nature, such as twigs and leaves

geometric—made of simple straight or curved lines

recycled—reused instead of being thrown away as trash

wicker—thin twigs used for making baskets and furniture

CREATE YOUR OWN MAKERSPACE!

1. Find a place to store supplies. It could be a large area, like the space in this story. But it can also be a cart, bookshelf, or storage bin.

2. Make a list of supplies that you would like to have. Include items found in your recycling bin, such as cardboard boxes, tin cans, and plastic bottles (caps too!). Add art materials, household items such as rubber bands, paper clips, straws, and any other materials useful for planning, building, and creating.

3. Pass out your list to friends and parents. Ask them for help in gathering the materials.

4. It's time to create. Let your imagination run wild!

MAKE A RECYCLED-ART ANIMAL SCULPTURE!

WHAT YOU NEED

- Craft glue or hot glue
- Markers, paint, paintbrushes, googly eyes, and other crafting materials (optional)

1. **Gather your found objects.** These may be items you find outside, such as twigs or seashells. They could be items in your recycling bin, such as plastic bottles, bottle caps, and newspaper. You might also find old toys, nuts and bolts, craft sticks, or other random items. Nearly anything could be useful!

2. **Separate your materials.** Divide your materials according to their uses. Which items could represent an animal's body or head? Which items might be used for legs, wings, or ears? Imagine a possible body part for each of your items to represent.

3. **Search for your idea.** Look through your items. Do any of them remind you of a certain animal? It is often easiest to start with body or head parts. For help, look at pages 25–27, where Matt is searching for his idea.

4. **Create your sculpture.** Arrange your found objects to look like the animal you chose. Then glue the items together.

FURTHER RESOURCES

Lim, Annalees. *Recycling Crafts*. New York: Gareth Stevens, 2014.

Miller, Shannon McClintock, and Blake Hoena. *A 3-D Printing Mission*. North Mankato, MN: Capstone, 2019.

Reynolds, Toby. *Junk Modeling*. New York: Windmill Books, 2016.

Venezia, Mike. *Pablo Picasso*. New York: Children's Press, 2015.

DON'T MISS THESE EXCITING ADVENTURES IN MAKERSPACE!

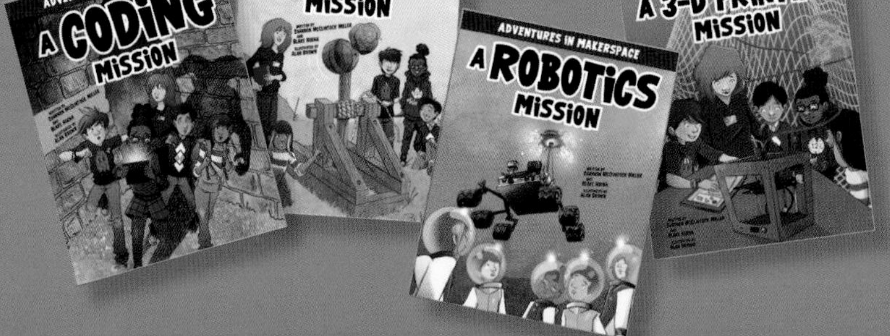

ADVENTURES IN MAKERSPACE
A CODING MISSION
ADVENTURES IN MAKERSPACE
A LOW-TECH MISSION
ADVENTURES IN MAKERSPACE
A ROBOTICS MISSION
ADVENTURES IN MAKERSPACE
A 3-D PRINTING MISSION